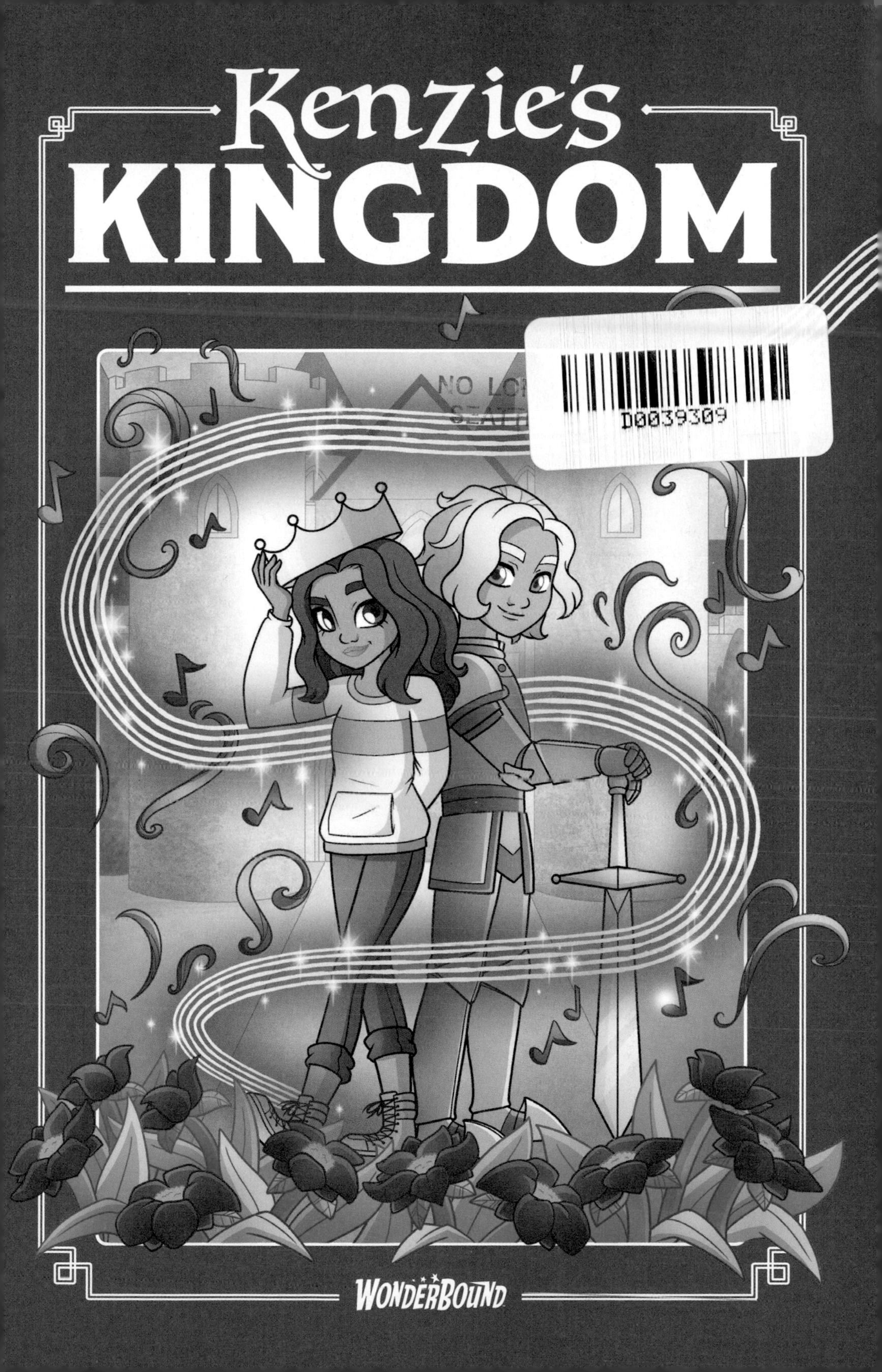
Kenzie's
KINGDOM
D0039309
WONDERBOUND

WRITTEN BY
SHEA FONTANA

ILLUSTRATED BY
AGNES GARBOWSKA

COLORED BY
SILVANA BRYS

LETTERS BY
GABRIELA DOWNIE

WONDERBOUND

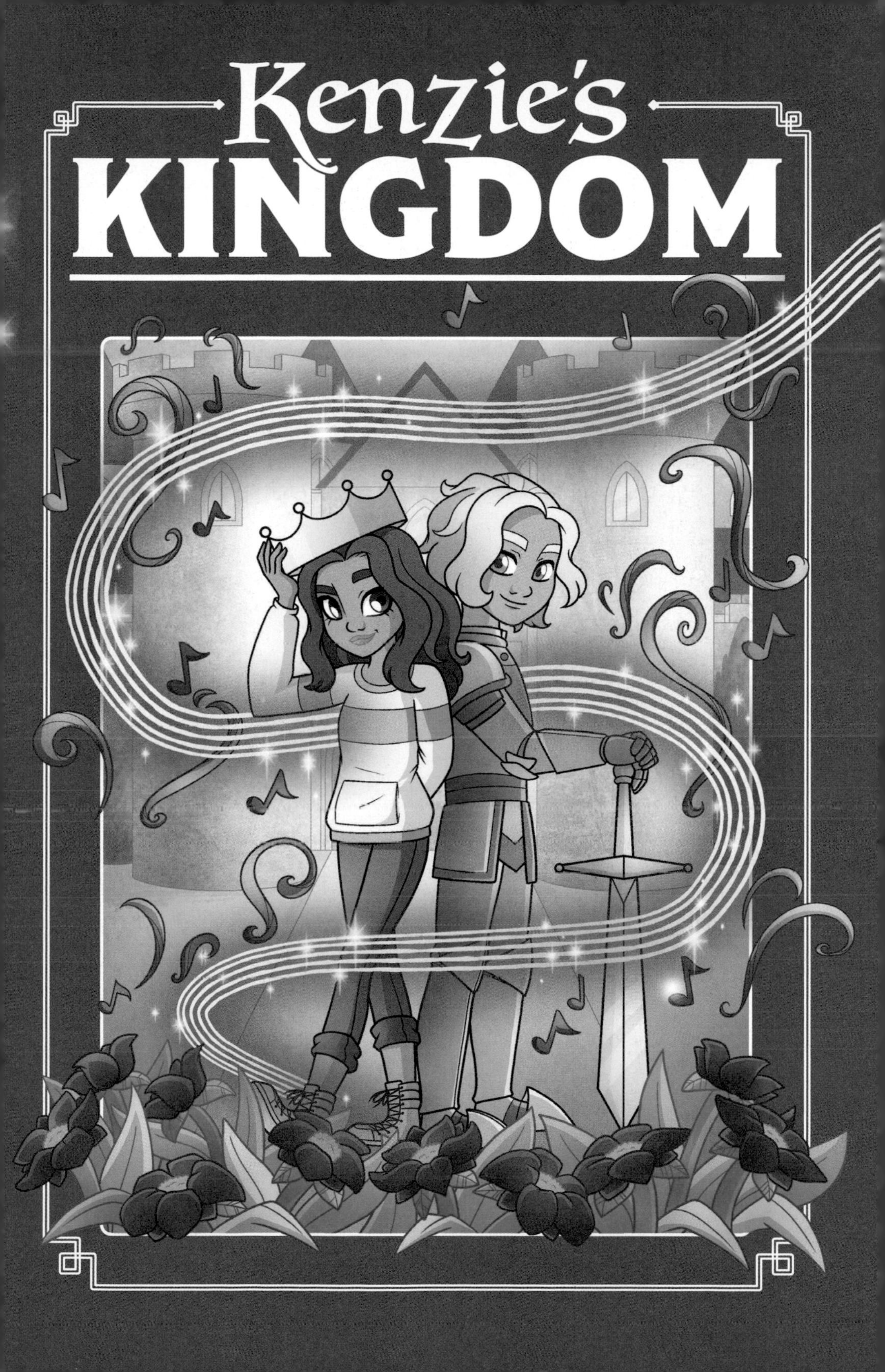
Kenzie's
KINGDOM

WRITTEN BY Shea Fontana
ILLUSTRATED BY Agnes Garbowska
COLORED BY Silvana Brys
LETTERED BY Gabriela Downie

EDITED BY Rebecca Taylor
DESIGNED BY Sonja Synak

PUBLISHER, Damian A. Wassel
EDITOR-IN-CHIEF, Adrian F. Wassel
SENIOR ARTIST, Nathan C. Gooden
MANAGING EDITOR, Rebecca Taylor
DIRECTOR OF SALES & MARKETING, DIRECT MARKET, David Dissanayake
DIRECTOR OF SALES & MARKETING, BOOK MARKET, Syndee Barwick
PRODUCTION MANAGER, Ian Baldessari
ART DIRECTOR, WONDERBOUND, Sonja Synak
ART DIRECTOR, VAULT, Tim Daniel
PRINCIPAL, Damian A. Wassel Sr.

Missoula, Montana
readwonderbound.com
@readwonderbound

ISBN:978-1-63849-072-2
LCCN:2021925251

First Edition, First Printing, July, 2022
1 2 3 4 5 6 7 8 9 10

Chapter 1
Once upon a time--
Help! Help!
Wait. That's not how I should start the story of that summer.
I'M in distress!
I'll save you, fair princess!
How about--

King's castle was full of dangers!
spider!
AAAAGGGH!
Trouble lurked around every corner.
Yikes!
Doom was in the air.

Peril crept on the stairs--
KLANK!
KLANK!
KLANK!
KLANK!
KLANK!
KLANK!
KLANK!
KING'S CASTLE
LUXURY RESORT
GRAND OPENING!
K
(And, wow, there are a lot of stairs in this old castle.)
KLANK!

It's a bad place for someone like me...Kenzie the Klutz.
Kenzie!
Oh fie.
Was that part of the show?
A girl knight? Hmph. That's not historically accurate!
You found Mr. Nibbles, my tarantula!
Wait. Maybe I shouldn't have started this story like that either.

I'm always **messing up** these kinds of things.
I can't believe I'M meeting *the* Rose King, the real Blubber Baby!
You were so cute in that commercial!
Thank you for the autograph!
In medieval times, they called it the "wolf spider."
Ew!
Now, *Frederick*, don't scare the guests.
One of our daughters loves the spotlight, and the other gets stage fright.
Since the show won't be going on, please accept this coupon for a free breakfast.
Make it two coupons--that was a disaster!
Sorry, everyone...for everything.
Because I am a mess.

How about I start here instead?
K
This is my family.
ROSE (Sister)
★ Starred in 26 Blubber Baby commercials before kindergarten.
★ Popular.
RALPH AND MARIE KING
(Dad and Mom)
★ Hospitality Professionals (that means they know all about hotels).
★ Love family adventures.
★ Think I need to "break out of my shell."
FREDERICK (Brother)
★ Super smart.
★ Won the California State Spider Fair.
KENZIE (Me)
★ Wants to go home.
★ Matching jacket didn't fit.
KING'S CASTLE
LUXURY • RESORT
Horseback riding! Archery range! Dinner shows!
The perfect place for the whole family!
And we just moved here--

--King's castle, Fralandia.
KING'S CASTLE
LUXURY RESORT
GRAND OPENING
BZZT
About a bazillion miles from my best friend, Aubrey, and California--my home.
BZZT
AUBREY
JUNE 1
Hey Kenzie! How's the castle? Monique and I went to this castle in your honor!
When my parents decided to move us here so they could start their own hotel, my dad called it a "fresh start."
How could a crummy old castle ever be fresh?
MURMUR
MURMUR

FWOSH!
The archery range is lovely!
I hope I can still get a riding lesson this afternoon.
HMMM
King's Castle
Arche
Rang
PLUNK!
Mom, save afternoon riding lesson appointment for Mrs. Barnes.
Oh, Kenzie, my sweet, shy girl.

My mom says the hospitality motto is, "My home is your home," but this place will never be my home.
What is that?
Yiii!
Oof.
Pardon me. Pray tell, who are the Lord and Lady of this castle?
THUMP!
Lord and Lady? You mean my parents?
Your parents? Oh, do forgive me my insolence, M'lady.

Squire Gavin of Oakwardshire at your service.
HUH?
Your Majesty.
Your what now?
Sorry, how do you prefer to be addressed, Princess?
Princess?
Princess it is then.

No, my name's Kenzie.
Princess Kenzie.
Just Kenzie.
Oh, I see! Princess Just Kenzie.
Is this a joke?
Most certainly not, but if you're in the mood for humor, please allow me to fetch your court jester--
Aagh!
THUMP!
Oof!
Oooh!

More like Gavin of Awkwardshire! I'll never be worthy of knighthood if I keep tripping over my two left feet.
It's okay. I'm super clumsy, too.
You are?
Yeah, watch this.
AyYi!
Princess! No!
Why'd you do that?!
It is my duty as a knight-in-training for King Edmunton the Fourth, long may he reign!
King Edmunton the Fourth? Wasn't that, like, five hundred years ago?

Five hundred years?!
I have heard the tales of traveling beyond the veil of time, but I never imagined being able to add my own story to them.
'Tis strange. This is my home--
HONK
HONK
Egad!
But it is very much not my home!
It's okay. I guess they didn't have bikes back then.
Take no offense, m'lady, but I would like to go home--
--to my true home, my family, and my friends.
Will you aid me on this quest?

I know I'm the girl who messes up, and I didn't want to make things worse, but I couldn't say no.
Of course, I wanted to help.
But everyone already thinks I'm a weirdo. I couldn't show up with a time-traveler!
So, I wanted to help, but secretly.
So, you really are a **knight-in-training** who traveled through time?
Yes. And you are a princess of the **Magic Kingdom** of Anaheim--
I'm from Anaheim, California, which is by... never mind.
But I'm most definitely **not a princess.**

Apologies. In my time, "princess" means that you own this space.
You belong.
You have power.
Ha! I don't have any power. I can't even be *where* I want.
Ah. Well, understood. I cannot even *be* what I want--
BZZT
BZZT

Hold on. I got a text.
You have...a "text"?
My parents let me get a phone so I can message my best friend, Aubrey, back home.
A device that allows communication from those who are, you said, a bazillion miles away?
Wonderful!
I have to reply. It's tough to find time to chat with the time difference and everything.
The time difference does make things difficult.
Uh-huh. This may take a sec. There's a lot going on there.
Take your time. As the knight I squired for would say, "Having a friend is easy.
"Being a friend is harder, but worth it."
BZZT
You probably have a bunch of friends, huh?
Well, my brothers are my dearest friends. I do miss them already.
BZZT

Right. So, we just have to figure out how to get you back where you belong...
While you think, we could go in, and I could light a fire to warm you.
I'm not cold.
But your thick garment.
It's not because I'm cold. It's just...
...Safe.
Ah, like armor.
Safe and shiny!
Shiny...wait! That light!
C'mon! I have an idea!

It was here. I saw a light coming from the flowers.
My knight told me these flowers are called *Travelers.*
Like *time travel.* There has to be a way to activate it--
Go flower power!
Time travel *ahoy!*
Bippity-boppity!
There's no place like home?
Oh, fie. These flowers aren't working!
Well, we must sleep.
Could we send a "text message" to the villagers and see if anyone would let me rest in their barn?
You... Uh...I... Umm...
You can stay here!

I know I am awkward, and I do not wish to be an embarrassment to yourself or your family. So, perhaps--
Huzzah! The old secret chamber remains!
Cool! I always wanted a secret chamber!
It's this way, m'lady.
Kenzie's **nerves** got the best of her again, huh?
?
Her anxiety's only gotten worse. Messing up the show is one thing, but I think she's even scared to talk to me, her own mother!
She threw this note, trying to help. She was being **kind,** but then she hid.
So much for a **fresh start.**
Kenzie?
This was my chance to finally do something right.
Coming, Gavin!
But could I do it without messing up?

Chapter 2
Good Morrow, Princess!
Zzzz--hmm?

Gavin? Wait, did anyone see you?
The garments you gave me from the Displaced and Findeth--
Lost and found.
They worked exceptionally well, and I was given nary a glance as I searched for your chambers.
I picked apples to break your fast.
Uh, thanks.
May I help you unpack?
KLCK KLCK KLCK
Nah. Less to re-pack when I go back home.
Kenzie Bags

Since I'm awake, might as well try to figure out how to get you back home.
I did have an idea on where we might find more information...
...the library! It is my favorite place in the whole castle!
LIBRARY
Frederick, out.
I was here first.
You can watch "Rollin' with Roland" in my room.
Fine...
Rolling with Roland?
It's this travel show my family is obsessed with.
...but who's he?
No one.
SLAM!

Okay, there has to be something on how to activate those traveler flowers so you can go back.
Get reading!
Sorry. I...can't read.
You can't read?
I love stories, books--
--but knights don't learn letters.
I am to focus solely on my knighthood training.
But, Princess, I must confess... for me, those feats of physicality come not naturally.
Here's a story you shall not find in these books--The Tale of Gavin the Nothing...

"In the kingdom of Fralandia, there was a boy from a family of knights, who was himself destined to be a knight.
"'Tis I. I am the boy.
FWIP!
"I squired for the best knight in the land.
Aaaagh!
"But I was still not adequate."
You have failed the Knight's Challenge.
I'm sorry, Princess Emeline.
You have two more chances. I believe in you, Gavin.
"I knew I had to pass the Challenge. I cannot read and am past the age to train as a blacksmith or baker. Being a knight is my only hope."

HA HA!
He didn't even get hit--he just fell!
We should call him "Gavin the Nothing"!
"But my *second* attempt was worse than my first."
KLUNK!
"Yesterday--er, *five hundred years ago yesterday*--was to be my *final* chance to pass."
GASP! GASP! GASP!
"But I couldn't even make it to the arena.
"I knew I wouldn't pass.
"When I opened my eyes, I was here. *Now.* And I--"
"Look!"

Is that the Princess from your time?
Emeline? Yes!
Princess Emeline
Welcomed all the travelers who came to the kingdom and helped them find their way. When the travelers got what they needed, they returned to their home
I think this is talking about the flowers!
Once you "get what you need," those traveler flowers will activate, and you'll go home!
You *need* to pass the Knight's Challenge, right?
Yes.
We can do that! Just one question--
What in the world *is* a Knight's Challenge?

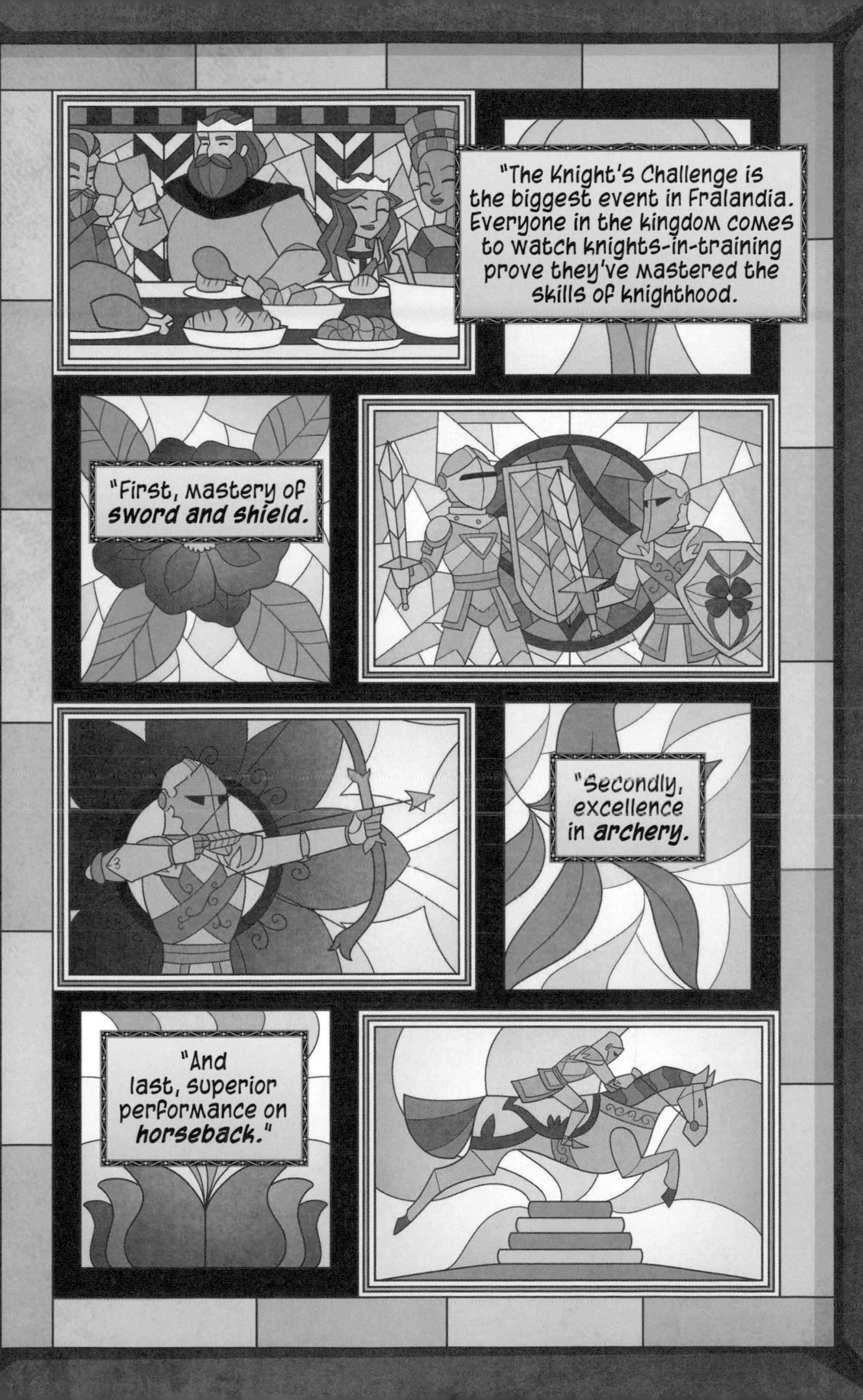
"The Knight's Challenge is the biggest event in Fralandia. Everyone in the kingdom comes to watch knights-in-training prove they've mastered the skills of knighthood.
"First, mastery of sword and shield.
"Secondly, excellence in archery.
"And last, superior performance on horseback."

Swords, archery, horses. It can't be that hard to learn that stuff, right?
Do you have a master of such skills here?
No, but I do know a sage...
We will learn from the Wise Wizard... *Internet-o!*
There's a lot of old stuff up here, even wooden training swords--
Careful, Princess.
STOP CALLING ME "PRINCESS"!
Rose, could you check on your sister before our riding customers arrive?
Sure thing, Mom.

Okay, Gavin...
Gahh!
THUNK!
PLUNK!
...let's fight!
Kenzie?
M'lady, I'm--
Rose, this is, uh, my new friend! From the village! Gavin.
PLUNK
Are you two sword fighting?
Umm...
Can I join?

No! It's just a silly thing, for only two people.
But I love stage combat--
Don't you have some **adoring fans** to get back to, Rose?
Yeah. My public awaits...
Who was that, Rose?
That's Kenzie's secret new friend from the village.
Aw! That's so wonderful! Our shy, little Kenzie making friends!
Now, to become the greatest knight Fralandia has ever known... and in record time!

INTERNET!

HOW-TO
COMICS!

'Kay, the video said to relax your fingers...
ARCHERY!
VOOSH!
You hit the target!
The high of five!
SMACK
Shall we?
HAHR!
Eep!
Whoa!
CRACK!
Princess!

Ugh! What's **wrong with me?**
There's nothing "wrong" with you.
The knight I squired for told me that when new to sword fighting, we try to make ourselves **small**, to **hide, disappear.**
But success comes when you learn to proudly **fill the space that you fill.**
"Fill the space that I--" Whatever that means.
BZZT
Gotta check that. Y'know, like that knight said, **"Being a friend is hard."**
Why did you not want your sister to join us?
I would've loved for my brothers to share such times.
Families are different than they were five hundred years ago. We don't really hang out.
But your family seems so nice and--
There's another shield inside that we can use. We need to focus on getting you back to your own time.

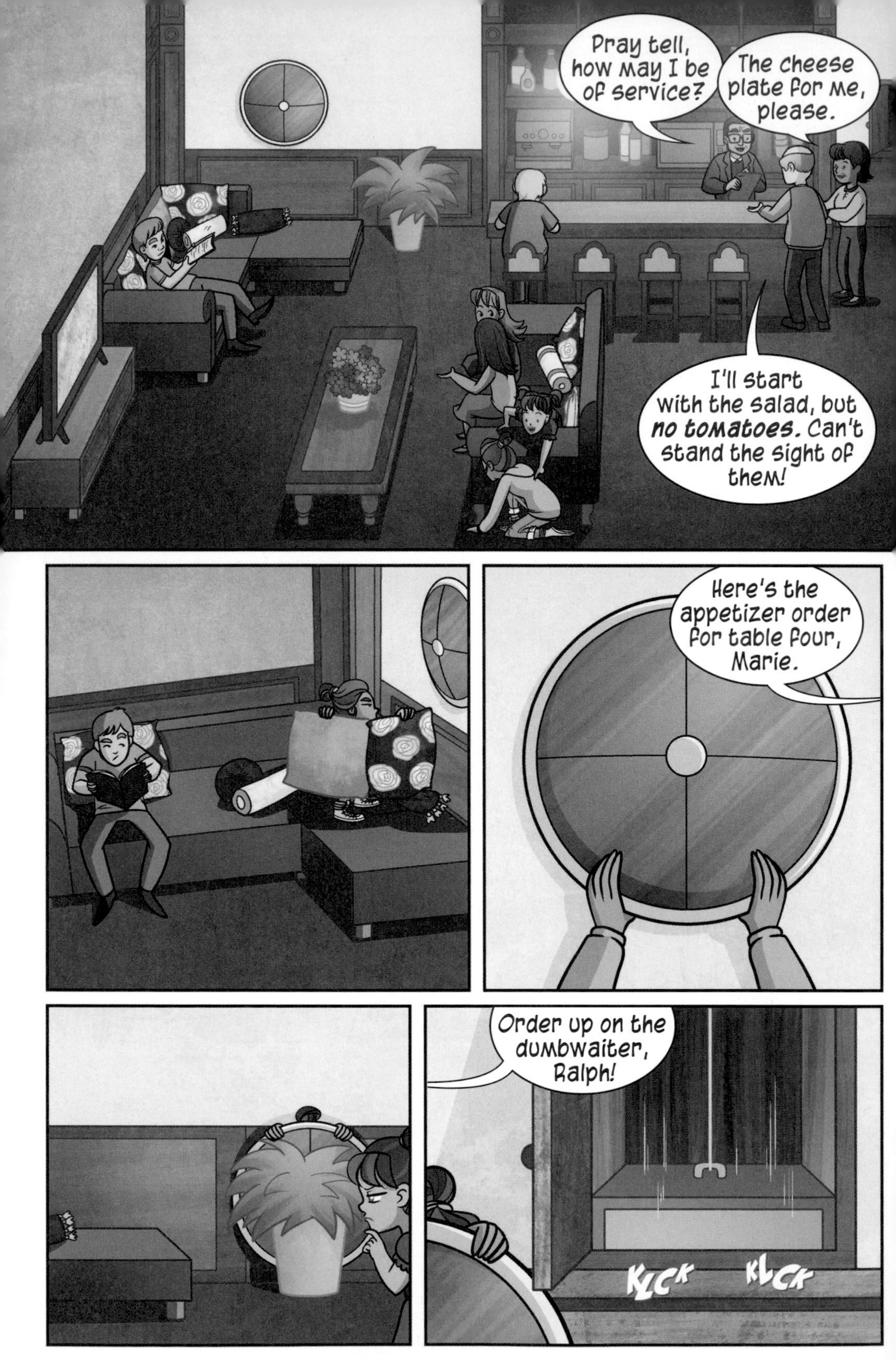
Pray tell, how may I be of service?
The cheese plate for me, please.
I'll start with the salad, but *no tomatoes.* Can't stand the sight of them!
Here's the appetizer order for table four, Marie.
Order up on the dumbwaiter, Ralph!
KLCK
KLCK

Rose, could you take that order to table four?
Sure, Dad.
Tomatoes?!
Stealthy helping success!
Aaagh!
Oof.

Oh my! Are you injured, Princess--
I am not the "Princess of Fralandia"! I don't even want to be *in* Fralandia!
But...it's *my fault* we're here.
A few months ago, I kinda freaked out at school.
"I couldn't breathe, and then everyone looked at me, and then I freaked out even more.
"It was like the world was closing in on me.
GASP
GASP
GASP
"It was like my brain was broken. Or my body was broken...
"...like I was broken."

That's why we moved.
I want to help you, Gavin, but I'll just mess everything up.
But you've already taught me so--
That's him!
I heard them! I heard everything--he's a *time traveler!*
Frederick, that's impossible.
UMMMM...
Before I could think of any excuse or explanation --
'Tis *quite* possible.
Pleased to properly make your acquaintance, young Prince and Princess. I'm Gavin of Oakwardshire.

So...Kenzie's helping Gavin learn how to sword fight, ride horses, and shoot arrows so he can pass this Knight's Challenge thing!
Then he can go back to his own time, which is five hundred years ago!
So, um, Rose. What do you think?
I think that's...
...AMAZING!
I can help! I have done so many stage combat classes!
I might be a mess, but Rose and Frederick aren't.
Maybe it won't be so bad if they know what's going on.

Maybe it won't be so bad at all.
You don't think this is weird?
Totally. But weird in the *coolest* way, Kenzie!
You activated a time-travel portal! That's amazing!
HUZZAH!
Maybe having Rose and Frederick around might actually be good.

Chapter 3
AUBREY
JUNE 3
Sorry I didn't reply! We were at the beach!
The gusto! Perfection!
KLUNK
Okay, the next step is to disarm your opponent.
Just a sec--
Does that count as disarming her?
BZZT

AUBREY
JUNE 15
What's up?
Not much. U?
babysitting the twins
Best one yet!
AUBREY
JUNE 28
Is that good?
Take it up to a trot.
GULP!
Woo!
Hey! Wait up!
Freddie, I can teach you to ride--
HUFF! HUFF!
I'm perfectly fine on my bike!
HUFF! HUFF!

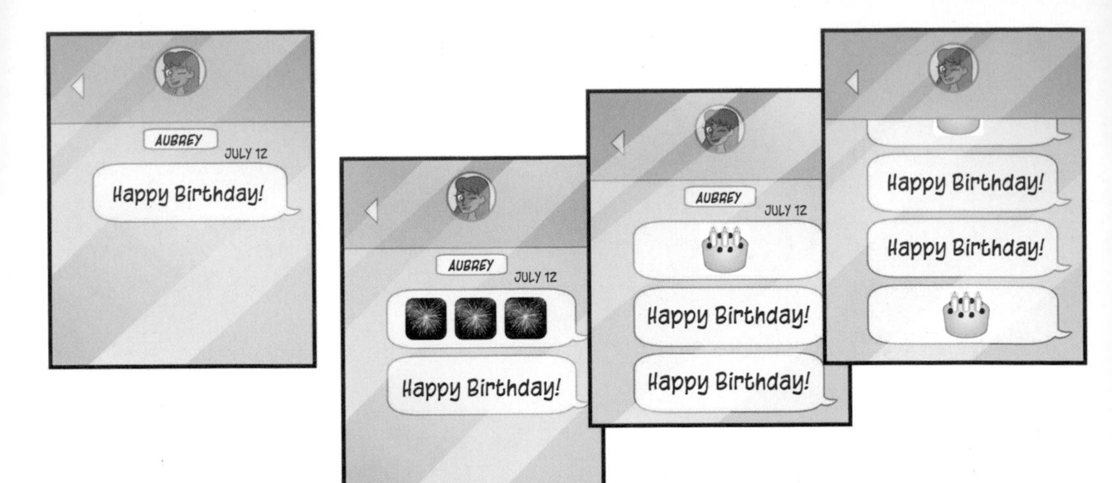
AUBREY
JULY 12
Happy Birthday!
AUBREY
JULY 12
Happy Birthday!
AUBREY
JULY 12
Happy Birthday!
Happy Birthday!
Happy Birthday!
Happy Birthday!

DRIP

K

THWAK
Wonderful!
I could do better-- if I weren't sweating so much.
ZIP
I haven't seen her without that sweatshirt on since fifth grade!
I haven't seen her without that sweatshirt on since fifth grade!

FWIP
THUNK
CLAP
CLAP
CLAP

CLAP!
Kenzie, Kenzie, that's her name, and shooting arrows is her game!
Huzzah!
Wowzers!
Um, thanks.
Atta girl.
Who would have thought?
AUBREY
August 9
called at 8 my time and your time. Where are you?

KLOP
KLOP
KLOP
High of the five!
SMACK
KLANG
Bravo!
Awesome!
As, Em--er, **my knight** would say, "You proudly fill the space that you fill."
Well done, Kenzie.

AUBREY
August 10
Meet you there
OOPS! Wrong number!
GIGGLE!
HA HA!
Are you sure about this, Kenzie?
Do it!

I could not imagine such a thing in my day with all the princess protocols.
At least the protocols made it easy to talk to strangers.
Like having a script. Takes some of the pressure off.
All a princess has to say is, "Hello," and "Welcome!"
VRRRROOooooOO
You know, Kenzie, you could try that, as a start.
Well...
Hello. I'm Kenzie. Welcome to King's Castle.

I've written up strategies for the Knight's Challenge.
I'll send them to the lobby printer so we can all see.
Remember to be quiet so we don't disturb the guests.
Or...maybe there's no one to disturb?
Knight strategies?
Yep! We love history, Mom!
Here are the most likely scenarios Gavin will meet during the Challenge.
Thank you, Frederick. But I can't--
I'll read them to you.
Almost as bad as a bed bug infestation!

This B&B gets a "roll on by" from Rollin' with Roland!
Oops. I thought I was turning up the volume in my headphones--
But you said wearing headphones while working was "rude."
That's only when there are guests...
KLCK KLCK
BOOKINGS:0
...and there are no bookings tonight.
Plus, the booking for tomorrow was canceled.
If business doesn't pick up before the end of summer...
SIGH
Coming up on the next episode of ***Rollin' with Roland,*** will Roland give this hotel in Thistlewood a "must stay" or a "roll on by"?

Thistlewood? I have a cousin who lives there. I would love to see--
We might as well all watch.
Keep your eyes peeled for anything that could help our business.
This building is two hundred years old--and it seems about that long since they've had a proper gardener!
That's Roland Hahn. He's a hotel critic.
This gentleman is quite rude.
That's what makes it good TV.
Look at them.
Here, Frederick. Blankie for your feeties.
Thanks, Kenz.

UNKOWN
555-8373
It's Aubrey. This is my MOM's phone. Noah dropped my phone in the ocean. I can't believe school starts in two weeks! 7th grade! I'll text you when I get a new phone, k?
Squire Gavin of Oakwardshire, you passed the Knight's Challenge and are hereby--
--KNIGHT GAVIN!
You've earned your sword, sir!
GHHHHH! I have been bested--*bested!*
If I can now pass the Challenge, then I got "what I needed," right? I can now return home?

Boo for you leaving us, but I'm so happy for you!
Goodbye, Princess Rose. I will cherish the time we've had together.
I made you this, so you can remember us.
TO: GAVIN
FROM: FREDERICK
Thank you, young Prince. I will miss your insight.
TO: GAVIN
FROM: FREDERICK
Kenzie?
But you can't leave until--

--We take one last horseback ride! Stupendous idea, Kenzie!
KLOP
KLOP
KLOP
Horse rides are fun, but you really can't go back until you've had a churro.
Chur-ro?
It's like cinnamon sugary heaven!
No one makes them around here.
But in California, you can get them everywhere--at the pier, theme parks, baseball games!
If business doesn't get better, maybe we could be back before baseball season's over.

Bases-ball sounds delightful, but I need to get home to my *family.*
But maybe you could stay until...
...the *holidays!* We make gingerbread houses.
My little brother, Johnny the Adorable, would love that.
His name is "Johnny the Adorable"?
Everyone in my family has a "*the.*"

Grandmother Gwendolyn the Bold. Uncle Peter the Courageous.
My father is Caleb the Strongarm, and my mother is Mary the Feast-Slayer.
I'm just Gavin the Nothing.
I get it. My family's soooo great.
Rose the Big-Talent, Frederick the Big-Brain...
SCOOT
...and Kenzie the Big-Mess.

Kenzie, you do have a great family.
And *you're* one of the greats.
Now, I have to go back to my time, my family, my friends.
And when I go back, I'll become
GAVIN THE KNIGHT!
I can't wait to show off my new moves to everyone back home!

There was nothing I could do to stop it. We had to say goodbye.
Though I trained with the best knight in the land, I was never able to master the skills needed to pass the Knight's Challenge until now.
I owe your whole family a great debt for that.
But especially you. Thank you, **Princess Kenzie.**
I told you...
...it's just "Kenzie."
Bye, Gavin.
Now, I'd be alone again.
Inhale--

AM I still here?
=Exhale=
YOU'RE STILL HERE!
Or maybe the forces of Fralandia wanted Gavin to stay with me forever!

Chapter 4
Ah, too bad, Gavin. Guess you're staying.
Now I can find a recipe for churros, and we'll make them, and--

I'm not in the mood for sweets.
It's not over forever, Gavin.
Now we have more time. There's probably something we missed for the Challenge. We can try again--
I *tried* my hardest. This is the best I've ever been.
And it's not good enough. *I'm* not good enough.
I want to be alone. I'll be in the *library* if anyone requires me.
But you can't even read!

HMPH!

I'll text you when I get a new phone, k?
Hey, Aubrey! Are you there?
TAP TAP TAP
HELLO?
TAP TAP TAP TAP
BZZT
Hi Kenzie! This is Janice, Aubrey's MOM. Aubrey is out with Monique. I'll have her text you from her new phone when she gets home. Tell your parents hi for Me!
She didn't text as soon as she got her new phone?
HYUCK!
SMASH
Kenzie?

Uh, you and Gavin want to do the archery demo?
Gavin's not my friend anymore. He doesn't want to stay with me.
And Aubrey doesn't care about me anymore.
I want to go home!
Sounds like we got a lot to unpack there.
Sweetie, I know it's been hard. But we're--
I just want to be alone, okay?
Okay. We're here when you're ready to talk.
I said I want to be alone--
Kenzie?

--Princess Emeline?!
A pleasure to meet you.
How...how did you get here?
Using the flowers is simple once you get used to it.

I hear you're having some trouble with my squire.
Your squire? You're the knight that Gavin's been talking about?
Yes, but it's a secret. Some in my day wouldn't approve.
He never said it was you!
Of course not. Gavin is a true, loyal friend.
Enough about me. I'm here to help you, Princess Kenzie.
I am not a Princess!

Hmph. A mistake then?
Probably. I make all sorts of mistakes, mess up everything.
Unfortunate.
Only the Princess of Fralandia can activate the flowers.
And only a true Princess can see what Gavin *really needs* to return home.
Wait. What?
I must go. And you must hurry, before the flowers cease to bloom.
Princess Emeline!

The flowers aren't always in bloom?
WOOSH
And here I am alone again...

...or maybe not.
Rose?
You okay?
No! It's...I... Ugh!
PLOP
Gavin didn't go because he didn't "get what he needs."
Oh, poor Gavin.
That's good!
But now I think I know what he really needs.
No, it's terrible. It means he'll leave.
Then I won't have **any friends!**

OOOoo
It's not like Freddie or I came here with friends packed in our suitcases either.
But you know *we're* your friends, right?
Really? I guess I felt like...
"...you're the big talent...
"...Frederick's the big brain...
"...and I was just... Kenzie."

Just Kenzie?
Kenzie, you notice everything, and you're the kindest person I know.
"You're the big heart that brings our whole family together."

Even though it's my fault that we had to come here?
Why would you say that?
Mom and Dad wanted me to have a fresh start.
They wanted us *all* to have a fresh start.
But you never mess up. Your *acting--*
Ha! I've gone on fifty-three consecutive auditions without booking a role.
I sorta had a "moment" last spring.
AUDITIONS
I don't want your stupid role anyway! I'm just here for the donuts!

Embarrassment city. Then there was Freddie's thing--
What?
"He lost his scholarship for the advanced studies program."
I had no idea. I'm sorry.
Eh, you had plenty of your own stuff to deal with.
So, are we friends or what?

Friends.
BZZT
Guess you need to get that?
Yeah... no...well. What I mean is that there are some things I *need* to do.
AUBREY
My new number! Wut up?
Okay, Miss Mystery, go do those "things."
I've been stuck in the past.
It's time to start thinking about the now.

Hi.
Hi.
EXIT
I was just looking at the pictures, imagining the stories...
Gavin, I'm sorry I haven't been a very good friend to you.
But, m'lady, you have been the best--
No, I haven't. I was only thinking of what *I* wanted, not what you really ***needed.***
It was like Princess--I mean--***your knight*** said...
"...Having a friend is easy. ***Being a friend*** is harder, but worth it."
I want to do the hard thing.
I'm going to ***teach you how to read.***
Really?!

Okay. First, the alphabet.
This is A, the first letter.
BZZT
Do you need to check your text?
It can wait.

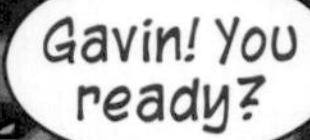

KENZIE

Hi, Aubrey. I'm sorry for being so demanding and cranky this summer. I wanted everything to stay the same, but it's not. I'm happy that you have other friends and aren't lonely. Someone really smart once told me that it was easy to have a friend, but hard to be a friend. I took the easy way. And now I need to make sure I'm being the best friend I can be to one of my new friends. But new friends don't take the place of old friends! We'll always be friends, too, okay?

"Dorothy lived in the midst of the great Kansas prairies..."
DOG! D.O.G.
D.O.G.
This was a show I watched when I was little.
TV pretty much taught me how to read, too.
Go on. You got this.
"H-he is m-my *dog*, Toto..."

I before E except after C and when it makes the sound of an A as in neighbor and weigh.
Rose, what are you wearing?
The costume helps me get into my Professor King character and--
Oh! Am I interrupting? They said that the library was open to guests...
I was just looking for something to read this afternoon.
Hi!
I'm Kenzie. Welcome to King's Castle.
I'll help you find what you need.

That's so cool.
Hi. Want to try?
Really?
You're in good hands. She's the best archer--and best teacher--in the kingdom.
"All you have to do is to knock the heels to-geh...together! Knock the heels together three times and command the shoes to carry you wherever you wish to go."

Chapter 5
"She was a vixen when she went to school; And though she be but little, she is fierce."
Again.
"Li...li-t-lee--ag...ag-a-i-n--"
Right. "Little again! Nothing but low and little!"
KING'S CASTLE
LUXURY RESORT

"Why will you suffer her to flout me thus?"
Are you talking to me?
It's Shakespeare, Dad.
WOLF BOY
Oh, Kenzie, you got a few cobwebs there. Better get them before school starts.
The Californians Abroad Online School is very demanding!
Daaad!
And how about you, Gavin? When does school in the village start?
Oh, um--

Actually, I go to boarding school.
I'll be leaving soon.
Well, I'm sad to hear that. You've practically become a part of the family this summer. In fact...
On this, the twenty-sixth day of August, I hereby proclaim Gavin to be an honorary member of the King family.
Go, Gavin!
HUZZAH!
TAP
Yes!
Do stay for TV time, Gavin. There's a new episode of **Rollin' with Roland** tonight.

I can't believe he said that.
GASP!
So salty.
It's not fair how he just shows up and surprises them like that!
Authentic Victorian paintings? Ha! My Aunt Victoria looks better, and she's been dead ten years!
You'll want to "roll on by" Mapleton Mansion.
What's that?
Working on my map-reading skills.
I've been plotting Sir Roland's travels.
Oh no! Look!

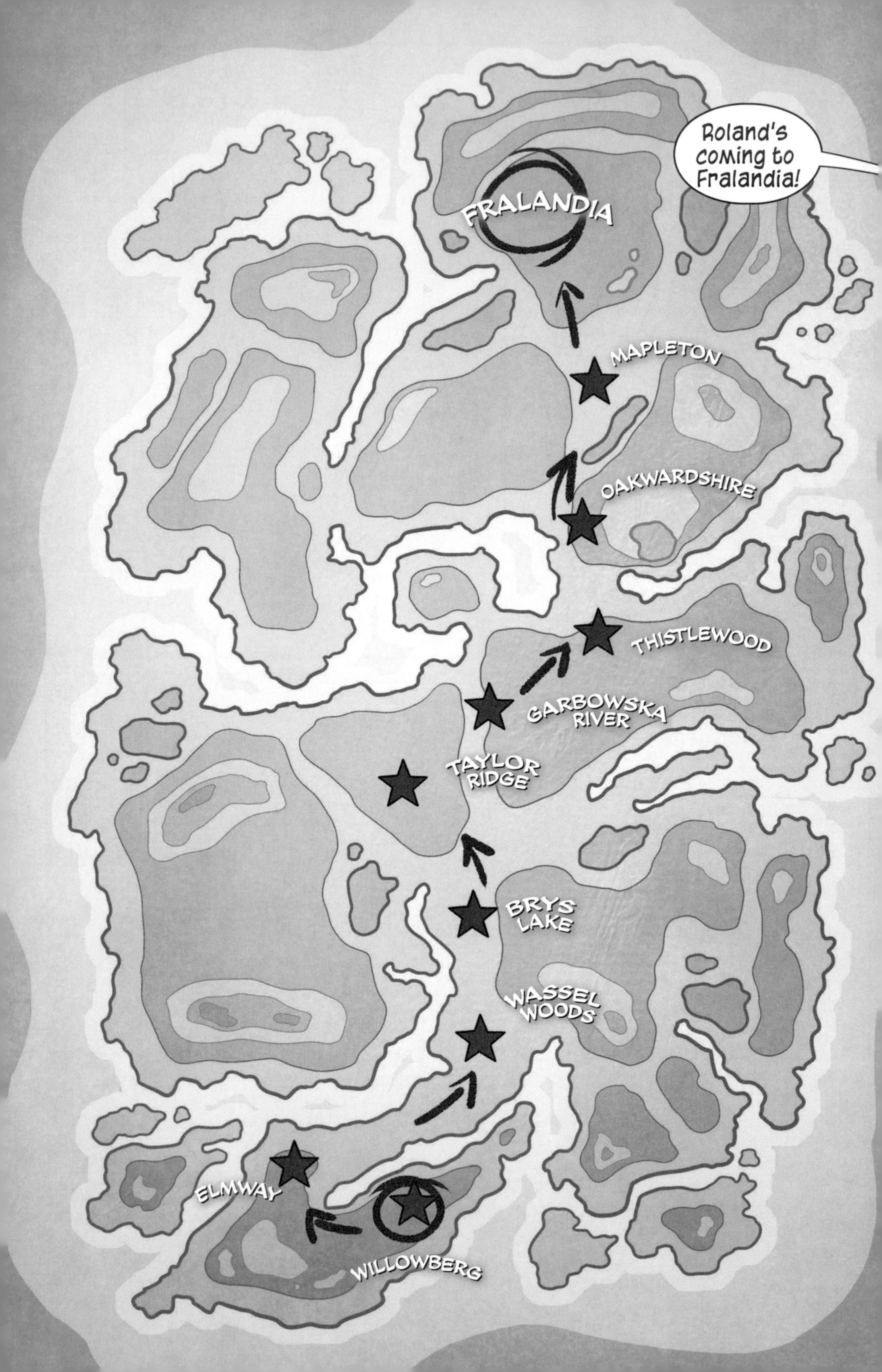

Roland's coming to Fralandia!
FRALANDIA
MAPLETON
OAKWARDSHIRE
THISTLEWOOD
GARBOWSKA RIVER
TAYLOR RIDGE
BRYS LAKE
WASSEL WOODS
ELMWAY
WILLOWBERG

According to my calculations, he'll be here **this weekend.**
I'm gonna be back on TV!
To our hotel?!
GASP! GASP! GASP!
A bad review from Roland would break the hotel.
If he embarrasses us, we'll have to give up the hotel, go back to California--
Dad.
It's okay. We're all here to help.
Okay, family! We're going to knock Roland's socks off!
I'm not sure he'd take well to the removal of his socks.
It's just an expression.

"Here's the plan--
"I'm good at noticing what people like and don't like."
The menu should reflect the land--
"I'll watch all of Roland's past episodes and figure out what we need to do to get a perfect review."
Accuracy and authenticity in historical depictions is a must!
zZZZZz
Roll-roll-rollin' through the countryside...
--Entertainment is key!

"Roland loves a good dinner show.
"The Knight's Challenge is the perfect, authentic event!
"Mom and Dad are working on the traditional recipes.
"Gavin, you know the challenge, and you're the best storyteller. You should do the script.
"Rose, you're on directing and costumes."
Frederick, you'll be playing the squire.
Rose, you're the princess.
Kenzie, you'll be a knight, along with me.
Gavin, this script is amazing. You're a writer!
"Roland will have to give us a good review!"

There you are!
Everything all right?
A little nervous about Roland coming tomorrow.
What's there to worry about? His stockings shall be removed!
You mean, we'll "knock his socks off."
Right! Knocked all the way across the kingdom!
Hahaha!

Even if it doesn't go well, you shall just return to the Kingdom of Anaheim, as you've wished.
'Tis a situation of what was called in my day, "winneth-winneth."
Does that ease your nerves?
...No.
But it's a different kind of nervous. Not the kind that used to make me want to hide.
I'm excited to do something new...because I know I can do it with you and my whole family.
We will welcome Roland to Fralandia and prove our knighthood.
As you wish, my *princess.*

I'll catch up. Just need to check on some things out here.
See you soon!
Ooooh! Brrrr!
Good evening, M'lady guest.
Ah! Good evening! Bit chilly, though.
WOOSH
And only getting colder!

Oh no.
WOOSH

Gavin!
You have to go tonight, while the flowers are still in bloom.
But the show--

We don't want to do the show without you, but we'll figure it out.
She's right.
You can't get stuck here. Your little brother needs you!
It's my **duty as Princess** to make sure you can go home. This is the hardest thing I've ever had to do, but...
...you have to leave before it gets too cold tonight and the flowers wilt.
Yes, your majesty.

Break a leg! That Means "good luck."
Don't forget us, okay, Gavin?
I am the Princess of Fralandia, and this traveler--
Wait.

Time will tell what your "the" will be, but to me, you'll always be ***Gavin, My True Friend.***
We're friends in the past, the future, and ***forever,*** Kenzie.

Read this before the show tomorrow.

I am the Princess of Fralandia, and this traveler has gotten what he needs. I command you to return him to his home.

Goodbye, Gavin.
Rose? Frederick?

Sniff!
Let it all out.
We're here for you, big sister.

Chapter 6
On this episode, will King's Castle earn a "must stay," or should you "roll on by" this historic hotel experience?
Now, it's time to surprise our hosts by popping in--
Welcome!
Huh?
What an astonishing--nay--*totally unexpected* surprise!

The key to the Ambassador's Suite!
Let me take your bag. I don't want you throwing out your back again.
Chamomile. Fresh from the garden.
Can I book an archery, sword skills, or horseback riding lesson for you during your stay?
A map of the grounds. I drew it myself!
Louise! Did you leak our itinerary?
Wasn't me. I think these folks are just that good.
For tonight's dinner show, we're presenting the Knight's Challenge--just like it was done five hundred years ago!
I'll be the judge of that.

Welcome, lords and ladies, to the Fralandia Knight's Challenge!
CLAP CLAP CLAP
Are you ready, Kenzie?
Um... almost.
Now, let's hear your finest "huzzah!"
HUZZAH!

Dearest Princess Kenzie,

Thanks to you, I have found my voice by learning letters. You are a true princess, a skilled knight, and, above all else, the best friend I could ever know. You own this space. You belong. You have power. Your family is rooting for you, and so am I.

Yours always,

GAVIN

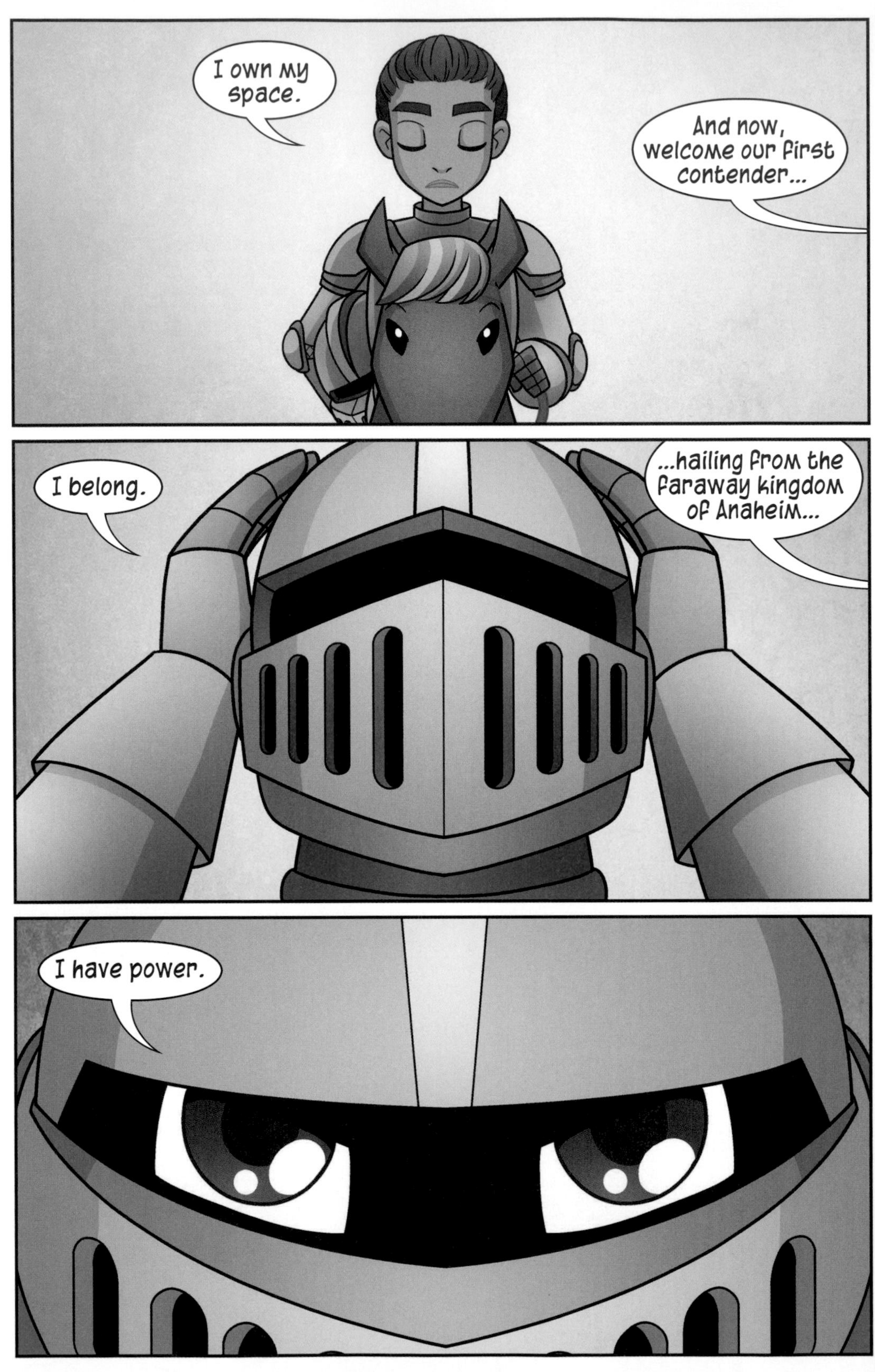
I own my space.
And now, welcome our first contender...
I belong.
...hailing from the faraway kingdom of Anaheim...
I have power.

It's ...Kenzie!
Neigh
But wait! Another contender?
CLAP
CLAP
CLAP
UMMMMM...
tremble
tremble
You got this, Freddie.
I am Frederick, and I'd like to be a knight, too, thank you.

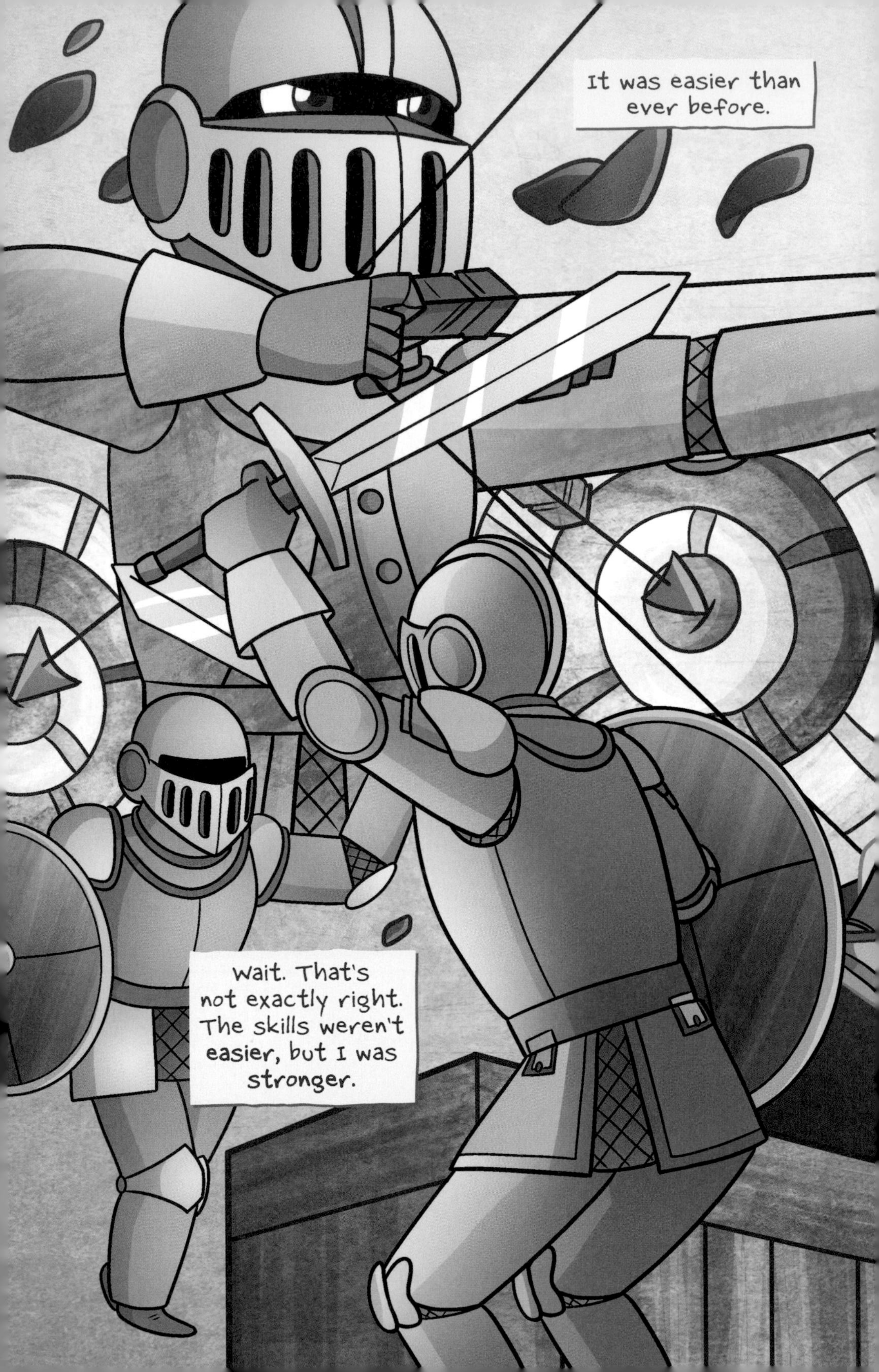
It was easier than ever before.
Wait. That's not exactly right. The skills weren't easier, but I was stronger.

Thankfully, I
wasn't a mess.
Because I'm
not a mess.

Kenzie King, I hereby proclaim you a Knight of Fralandia.
Hmph.
Huzzah! Three cheers for Kenzie the Knight!
HIP HIP...
...HOORAY!

CLAP
HUZZAH!
CLAP
CLAP
Those are our kids!
Woo!
CLAP CLAP CLAP
Phenomenal!
Give Kenzie a boost!
KenZie!
KenZie!
KenZie!

Louise, my good side, please--
Sir Roland!
I hope you enjoyed your dinner as much as we enjoyed hosting you at our *home.*
It was spectacular! I've never seen such historical accuracy.
How did you do it? It's like you traveled back in time!
Oh, well, *something like that.*

C'mon, Freddie. Let's get the horses to the stable.
Can you believe how loud they cheered, Rose?
I'm heading in!
Great work tonight, Kenzie!
We're so proud of you!
You would have loved it, Gavin.
Do you work here?

Oh, hello! Yes, how can I help you?
Sorry to intrude. We've been backpacking across the country.
We'd be happy to sleep in the barn or under the stars--
If we had your permission.
Travelers are *always welcome* in Fralandia.
And I can do *better* than a barn.
Wow! But let us work to earn our keep.
Any odd jobs around the castle?

Actually, I could use some help.
We have this old greenhouse that needs to be repaired. I want to *garden* in it this fall...
KING'S CASTLE
LUXURY RESORT

King's Castle is a "MUST stay," the Roland way! With so much to do at this resort, you'll want to book a whole week.
KING'S CASTLE
LUXURY RESORT
So, the show was a big hit. We do it every night now.

We're booked all the way through the holidays.
Smells incredible!
The King family tea. My sister grows the herbs in the greenhouse.
I found six different spiders just today!
Whoa. Cool!
How was your stay?
But even though we'll be busy, Mom and Dad said we'll still make gingerbread houses.
Phenomenal! I only regret we couldn't stay longer.
Hey, Kenzie!

I don't know why I keep writing you.
Yes, Mom?
Could you put these back in the library?
Good morrow.
Hello!
LIBRARY
Maybe one day, another time traveler will appear, and I can send these letters back with them.

LIBRARY
Or maybe I'll figure out how to go back myself.
TRAINING SHIELD OF A 16TH CENTURY KNIGHT
TRAINING SHIELD OF A 16TH CENTURY KNIGHT
I keep writing, just in case we find a way to communicate five hundred years apart.
Or...

...maybe you already figured it out!
Princess Kenz
the Kindheart
Gasp!
The First Tale of
Princess Kenzie
the Kindheart
Written by
Gavin the Storyteller
Bard of Fralandia

"It was difficult for the young princess to see herself like others saw her...
"...as she trained, her power grew...
"...the greatest knight Fralandia had ever seen...
"...together, the family defeated cruel Sir Roland!
"Though she was fierce of body, Princess Kenzie's greatest strength was her generosity of spirit.
"That's how she changed the world and became known as Kenzie the Kindheart."

Wow, Gavin's got talent.
Read it again!
Until next time, my friend,
Princess Kenzie

ABOUT THE CREATORS

SHEA FONTANA

is a writer for film, television, and graphic novels. She is currently showrunning the new *Monster High* series for Nickelodeon and Mattel. Her credits include developing and writing the *DC Super Hero Girls* animated shorts, TV specials, movies, and graphic novels; *Polly Pocket* (developed, executive story editor, creative producer), *Doc McStuffins*, *The 7D*, *Whisker Haven Tales* with the *Palace Pets* (wrote show bible and first season), *Dorothy and the Wizard of Oz* (story editor), and *KindiKids*; two Disney on Ice shows, where she wrote new material for the worlds of Mickey Mouse, Inside Out, Disney Princesses, Finding Dori, Frozen, and other Disney and Pixar properties; and the feature film *Crowning Jules*. She has also written for top comic titles including *Justice League*, *Wonder Woman*, *Batman: Overdrive*, *Catwoman/Looney Tunes*, and contributed anthology pieces starring Deathstroke and the Teen Titans. Her first non-fiction book is *DC: Women of Action*, published by Chronicle. Her graphic novels have been New York Times Bestsellers.

AGNES GARBOWSKA

was born in Poland and came to Canada at a young age. Being an only child she escaped into a world of books, cartoons, and comics. She currently lives in the States and enjoys sharing her office with her two little dogs. Agnes is best known for her work on *DC Superhero Girls*, as well as *Teen Titans Go!* for DC Comics. She has worked for IDW Publishing, illustrating *My Little Pony*, *Care Bears*, and *Jem and the Holograms*. At Marvel Comics, she has provided artwork for *Girl Comics* and *Spider-Ham 25th Anniversary Special*, as well as cover art for *Marvel's Super Hero Adventures*. Her work expands to other companies including Archie Comics, Oni Press, Boom!, Dynamite Entertainment, and Aspen Comics.

SILVANA BRYS

is a colorist and graphic designer who has colored *DC Super Hero Girls*, *Teen Titans Go!*, *Scooby-Doo*, *Scooby-Doo Team-Up*, *Tom & Jerry*, *Looney Tunes*, *Carebears: Unlock the Magic*, and many other comics and children books for different companies. She lives in a small village in Argentina. Her home is also her office, and she loves to create there, surrounded by forests and mountains.

GABRIELA DOWNIE

is the daughter of Central American refugees, born and raised in the heart of Los Angeles. She has two black cats that appear when summoned and can talk to plants. She has invisible devil horns that hold up her brilliant halo, and what seems like a Cintiq pen in her hand is actually the deadliest sword ever crafted.